SADIE'S
sea turtle

SADIE'S
sea turtle

Copyright © 2021 by Dove Publishing

Written by Chris Elle Dove
Illustrated by Sofie Schollaert
Edited by Wildflower Books

For more information, contact Chris Elle Dove at ChrisEDove@gmail.com
ISBN 978-1-7363598-0-8 (paperback)
ISBN 978-1-7363598-1-5 (hardcover)
ISBN 978-1-7363598-2-2 (e-book)

I'm incredibly thankful for, and would like to recognize:

James and Nicole, my amazing children, who've provided all of the raw material and inspiration
I'll ever need for my picture books.
The man of my dreams, who listens intently to my endless ramblings about my writing.
My illustrator Sofie Schollaert, whose images breathe life into my words and characters.
Jeff Jaeger, Shannon Jade, and Marina DelVecchio, for offering editorial suggestions and advice.
And my "tiny beta testers" who always provide a wealth of insightful feedback.

Many things made Sadie smile. For instance, the sea.
She hadn't been there for a while, not since she was three.

She dipped her toes in the sand and collected shells.
She danced to a steel drum band and smelled salty smells.

Sadie built mighty castles
and soaked up the sun.
Splashing, crashing, and dashing
through breaking waves was fun!

Sadie chased after a towel
that the wind blew away.
Before she left, she promised
"I'll be back again someday."

Since Sadie had returned home, her curiosity had grown.
She'd sought out every bit of knowledge there was to be known.

Sadie read lots of books and worked with her teachers.
She learned all about the most amazing sea creatures.

The field trip to the zoo with Miss May was the best.
She took Sadie's class after they all aced a test.

That's where Sadie learned
seahorses like to swim in pairs.
And of all animals,
sea otters have the most hairs.

Carpet is a type of shark.
Jellyfish glow in the dark.
Pinfish have a distinct mark.

All day long, jumbo squids park.
Electric eels shock and spark.
Sea lions grunt, growl, and bark.

An oyster can make a pearl in pink, white, or gray.
Octopus tentacles curl to hold onto prey.

Dolphins don't chew their food. They simply swallow.
And stingrays in a bad mood aren't good to follow.

Though not overly fast, sea turtles are a blast.
Though not unusually smart, they had space in Sadie's heart.

Sea turtles come in
gray, black, brown, green, and gold.
And they can, by the way
live to be quite old.

Plastic DANGER

Be...of plastic in the oceans, sea turtles are being hurt. They get entangled in fish ropes or plastic bags. One time use plastic items should be banned from our daily lives. There are many more sustainable alternatives.

...the sea turtle population is under an i... ...ssure, sea turtles sometimes d... ...e ropes and can not fr...

When she realized sea turtles were being hurt,
Sadie grew quite sad, then went on high alert.

One threat to sea turtle safety
is plastic pollution.
Sadie wanted to become
a part of the solution.

Sadie picked up litter found on the sidewalk,
wrappers in the playground, and trash near her block.

Leaving pieces of litter on the ground is rude,
even if sea turtles don't mistake it for food.

Though Sadie did collect
a lot of icky stuff,
she started to suspect that
it would never be enough.

"Let's help the community!" Miss May declared.
For this opportunity, Sadie prepared.

The students got into groups to work on Sadie's plans.
They ran through town in loops, grabbing cups and cans.

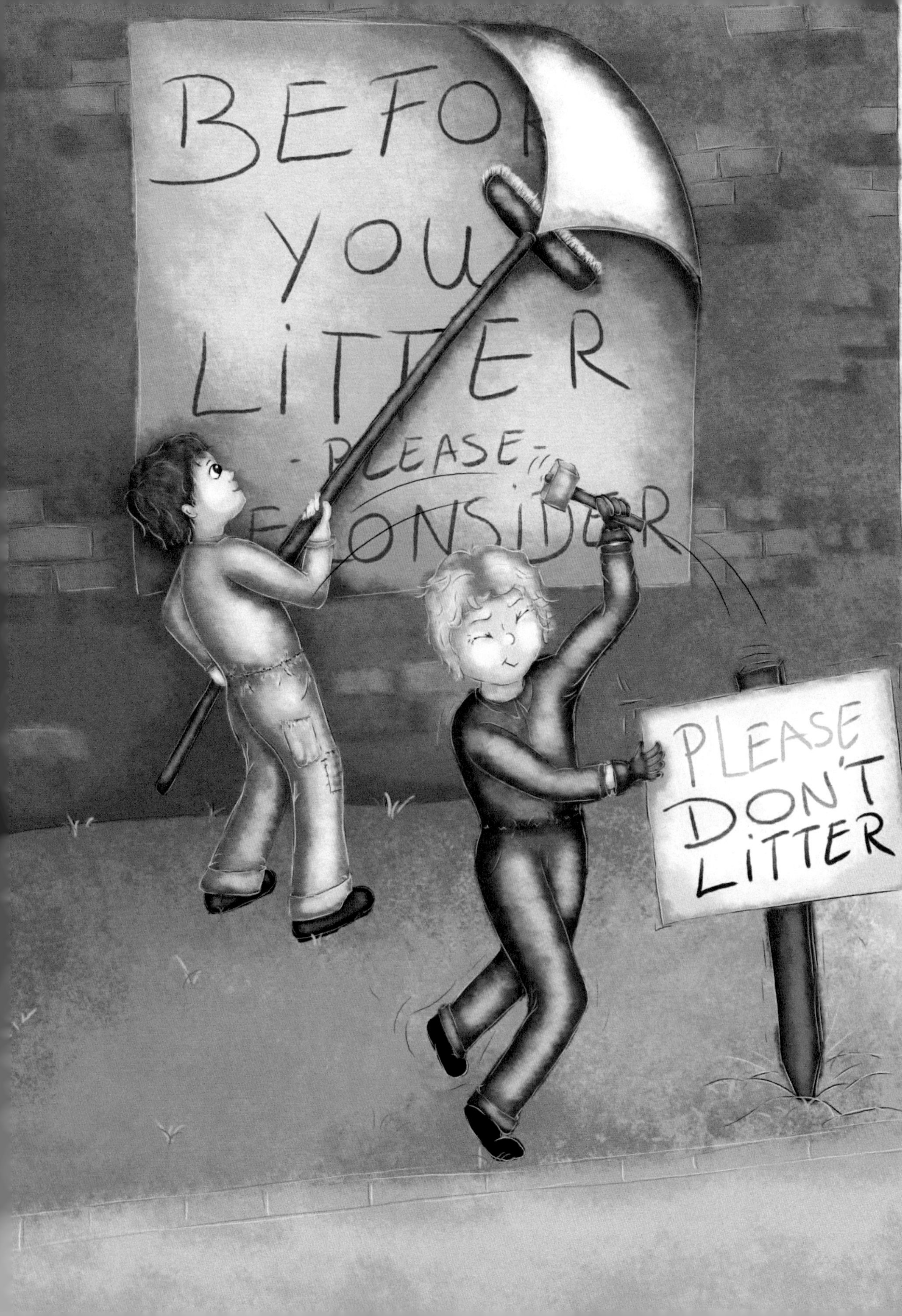
BEFO
YOU
LITTER
- PLEASE -
CONSIDER
PLEASE DON'T LITTER

Logan made a sign that said, "Please, don't litter!"
Ethan's read, "Before you litter, please reconsider!"

Many lent a hand to keep the town neat.
Lily thought it would be grand to help for a treat.

Some saw saving turtles as the right thing to do.
Because of Sadie's pizzazz, the cause grew and grew!

Miss May was surprised.
Although she'd barely advised,
the entire town was energized!

Although slightly dazed,
Sadie's teacher was amazed.
She said to herself, "Sadie should be praised!"

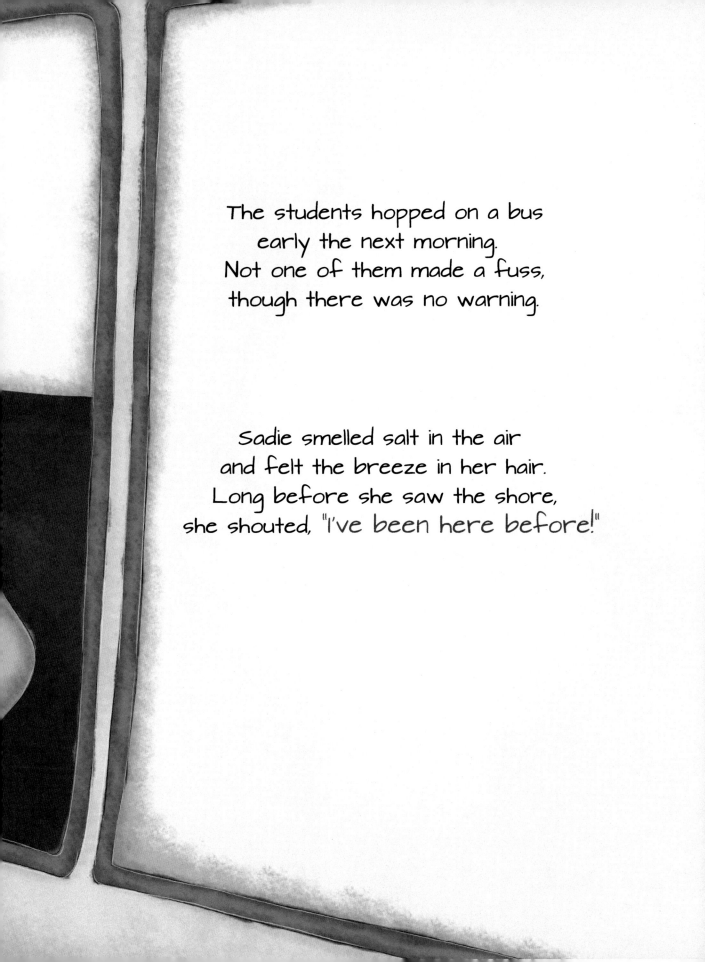

The students hopped on a bus
early the next morning.
Not one of them made a fuss,
though there was no warning.

Sadie smelled salt in the air
and felt the breeze in her hair.
Long before she saw the shore,
she shouted, "I've been here before!"

The sand on the beach
was sprinkled with something small.
There, baby sea turtles
were learning how to crawl!

Miss May asked Sadie, "See that one right there?"
Sadie nodded.
Miss May said, "There's something you two share."

"What could it be?" said Sadie.
"There's nothing I can see."

"The turtle and me?
I may disagree."

Sadie, stumped, just had to ask,
"How can that be true?"
Miss May responded with glee,
"She was named after you!"

The End

More...

Download more activities at ChrisDoveWrites.com

Made in the USA
Middletown, DE
10 July 2023

34851040R00024